Mimi's First MARDI GRAS

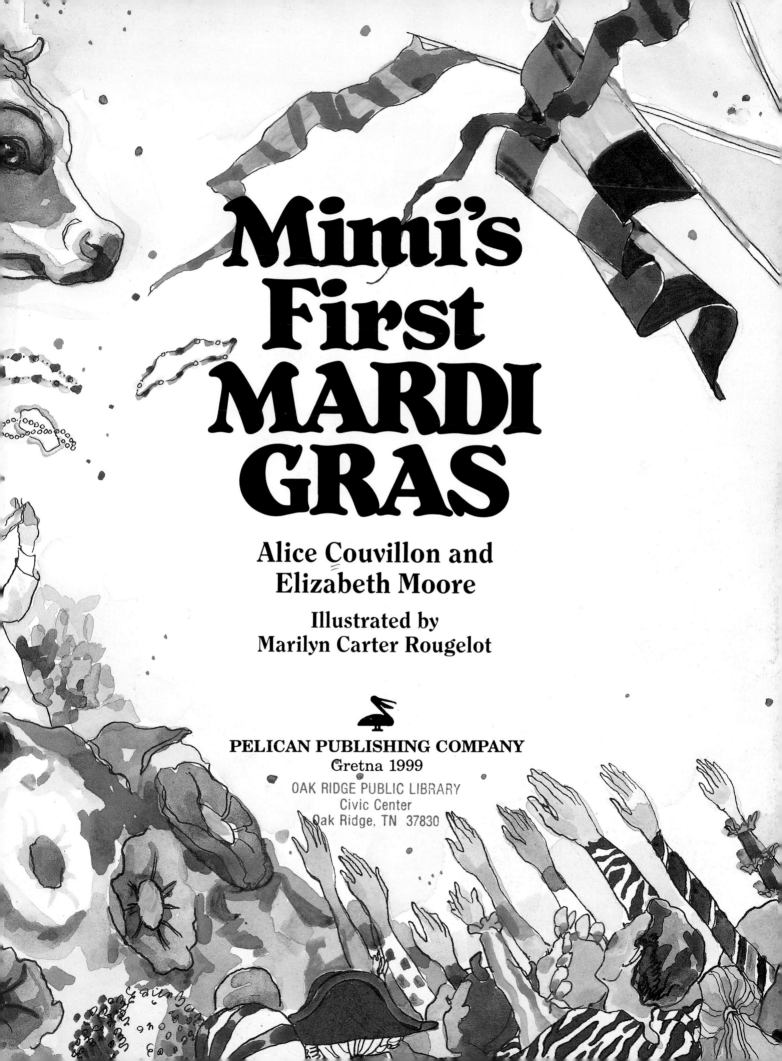

Mimi's First MARDI GRAS

Alice Couvillon and Elizabeth Moore

Illustrated by
Marilyn Carter Rougelot

PELICAN PUBLISHING COMPANY

Gretna 1999

First printing, January 1992
Second printing, November 1995
Third printing, February 1999

In gratitude to . . .

Gloria Crassons, whose idea inspired this book

our husbands, Robert Couvillon and Richard Moore, for their good-natured support for another one of our projects

our children, Ginny, Emily, Meg, and Caroline Couvillon and Sarah, Miriam, Jefferson, Patrick, Sean, and Jody Moore, for helping us see Mardi Gras through their eyes.

Library of Congress Cataloging-in-Publication Data

Couvillon, Alice.
  Mimi's first Mardi Gras / Alice Couvillon, Elizabeth Moore; illustrated by Marilyn Carter Rougelot.
      p.   cm.
  Summary: Mimi and her parents enjoy the color and excitement of Mardi Gras in New Orleans and observe many traditional aspects of the celebration.
  ISBN 0-88289-840-X
  [1. Carnival--Fiction. 2. New Orleans (La.)--Fiction.]
I. Moore, Elizabeth. II. Rougelot, Marilyn Carter, ill. III. Title.
PZ7.C8334Mi 1992
[E]--dc20   91-24006
                                                      CIP
                                                       AC

Printed in Hong Kong

Published by Pelican Publishing Company, Inc.
1000 Burmaster Street, Gretna, Louisiana 70053

MIMI'S FIRST MARDI GRAS

Mimi's mother kissed her on the forehead.

"Mimi, it's time to wake up. Today is Mardi Gras!"

Mimi's eyes popped open and she gave her mother a big smile and hug. Ever since twelve days after Christmas, Mimi had been dreaming about the fun and excitement of Mardi Gras.

On Twelfth Night, Mimi's parents gave a party. The highlight of the evening was the cutting of a very special cake, called a King Cake. Shaped like a huge ring, the cake was iced in the Mardi Gras colors of purple, green, and gold. Hidden inside one of the slices of the cake was a tiny baby doll, and whoever got the slice with the baby was expected to give the next King Cake party. The parties continued until Mardi Gras day. Everytime Mimi went to a King Cake party, she knew that Mardi Gras was getting closer and closer.

Mimi slipped on her cuddly robe and skipped into the kitchen. As she sat in a chair, her mother placed a platter of sizzling beignets on the table.

Mimi and her parents quickly ate the crispy, square doughnuts that Mother fried for every holiday breakfast. Her father picked one of the hot, puffy beignets which had been sprinkled with powdered sugar and took a big bite. Mimi giggled as clouds of sugar covered him from tip to toe.

"Oh Daddy! You already look like you have your clown makeup on!"

Her father smiled and said, "All I need is my big red nose and I'll be ready for Fat Tuesday."

"Fat Tuesday! What is that?" Mimi asked.

"Mardi Gras is French for Fat Tuesday," her father explained.

Mimi wondered, "Why is it called Fat Tuesday?"

"Well, Mardi Gras is the last day before Ash Wednesday, which begins Lent. During this time, we fast, which means to eat less. We also give up something we like to do, like going to parties or movies, and we try to go to church more often. So, on Mardi Gras people 'eat, drink, and be merry' for the last time before the forty days of Lent. So you can see why Mardi Gras is called Fat Tuesday."

"Forty days is a long time," said Mimi.

"Yes, and guess what celebration ends the forty days of Lent? It's Easter!"

"Oh," said Mimi, "Lent begins with a fat day and ends with a fat day, too." And she licked her lips as she thought of the delicious chocolate eggs and bunnies in her Easter basket.

"Mimi, it's getting late," Mother called. "The parades begin early, and we have lots to do to get ready."

Mimi's parents dressed as clowns, and they had wanted Mimi to be a little clown, too, but Mimi had her heart set on being a beautiful princess. Her mother had carefully sewn a princess costume. Mother pulled the dress over Mimi's head and helped her button it up.

Mimi jumped with delight. "Mommy, it's so pretty. I feel like a real princess."

The ruffly blue skirt was trimmed with delicate lace, and she wore a jeweled crown that twinkled like the stars. Mother brushed pink color on Mimi's cheeks and dabbed a little lipstick on her lips. Mimi's eyes glistened and her cheeks glowed, and she felt as sparkly as her crown.

Mimi smiled as she got into the car. She had never seen a clown drive before, and when they turned onto St. Charles Avenue, she noticed a family of gorillas step into the streetcar. Mimi knew that it would be a funny time.

"Daddy, are gorillas on the trolley in San Francisco where Aunt Boo and Uncle Tucker live? Are they going to a Mardi Gras parade today, too?"

"No, honey, Mardi Gras is celebrated in only a few places. You see, the French people who settled here brought the tradition of Mardi Gras with them. And in New Orleans, we continue this custom every year."

"We're really lucky to live here, aren't we?" Mimi exclaimed. "It's fun to be silly for a day."

The traffic got heavier, and the car slowed to a crawl. "Daddy, we'll be late for the parades. Our car is hardly moving at all."

"You're right, Mimi. But I know a special route. We'll be there in a blink of an eye."

Father turned off at the next street. Pressing her nose against the car window, Mimi stared at the people with painted faces and funny clothes. Then she saw a group of men dance by, shuffling and twirling like giant birds. Tiny beads in fancy designs decorated their costumes and pink, purple, blue, and yellow feathers waved from their headdresses and trailed down their backs. They flapped their arms like wings, and Mimi said, "Daddy, look at those big birds. I think if they flapped their wings enough, they would fly away."

"Those aren't birds, Mimi. That's a group of Mardi Gras Indians. Different groups of black men form tribes and give them names like 'White Cloud Hunters,' 'Wild Magnolias,' 'Creole Wild West,' and 'Yellow Pocahontas.' It's a very old tradition, maybe two hundred years old. The men work an entire year on their costumes, carefully sewing on the beads and feathers in their own design. On Mardi Gras they dance in the streets and meet up with other tribes. When the day is over, they cut off and save all the beads and feathers and start planning their costumes for next year."

They heard the pulsing drums start beating, and the Indians formed a circle, clapped their hands, and called to each other:

I-ko, I-ko, I-ko, I-ko-ah Nay
Chokamo, Feenah, Ah Nah Nay
Chokamo Feenah Nay.

Mimi saw many colorful maskers as they drove along, but she thought that the Mardi Gras Indians were the most wonderful of all.

But, where was the parade?

"Daddy, I've blinked my eyes a lot. Where's the Mardi Gras?"

"Right here, Little Princess. We'll have to walk a bit, but it is impossible to park any closer on Mardi Gras day." And although it was a very long way, it was fun to see people dressed as crawfish, rag dolls, Gypsies, and cavemen.

They heard the sounds of a   jazz band and watched men in tuxedoes twirl decorated umbrellas as they moved to the music. Someone in the group handed Mimi a flower from a giant bouquet and kissed her on the cheek.

"Let's second-line to the parade!" her father said, and Mimi and her parents danced behind the spinning umbrellas.

When they stopped in the middle of the avenue, Mimi was puzzled. "We're not supposed to play in the street."

"You're right," her mother answered, "but everything is different on this day. Just stay close. Zulu is coming soon."

"Who's Zulu, Mommy?" Mimi asked.

"Zulu is a parade. It's an African-American group that has been around for more than seventy-five years. Early in the morning the king arrives by barge on the Mississippi River and joins his krewe for the first parade on Mardi Gras day. One year Louis ('Satchmo') Armstrong, a famous jazz musician who played the trumpet, was the king."

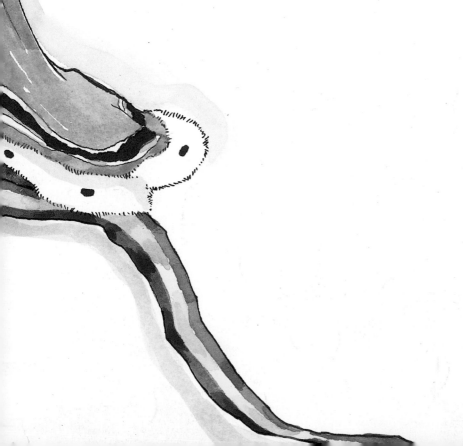

Someone cried out, "Here it is! Here comes the parade!"

The crowd closed in, and Mimi felt very small and a little afraid, but her father lifted her up and sat her on his shoulders. Even though she was high above the crowd, the parade was still too far away to see, but she could hear the sirens in the distance.

She held tighter to her father's chin and bounced up and down on his shoulders as the screaming sounds grew louder. Mimi clapped her hands over her ears while the motorcycles roared by.

Then she heard the clip-clop of horses' hooves as the mounted police sat proudly on their gleaming saddles. The horses whipped their long, silky tails and pranced before the band majorettes who marched and danced to the music. One girl swirled a flag, but the others had long, silver batons that they twirled around their fingers and threw high into the air. When the band marched close to Mimi the drums boomed so loudly that they tickled her tummy.

Then the floats moved down the avenue one after another. Zulu's members dressed like African tribesmen in grass skirts and leopard skins, and their faces were blackened with white circles painted around their mouths and one eye. To the outstretched arms below, they threw trinkets and beads and passed out strange golden balls decorated with a sparkling *Z*.

"Coconut! Coconut!" someone yelled, and the crowd took up the cry and chanted in unison, "Co-co-nut! Co-co-nut!" Everyone screamed as they waved their arms wildly and jumped for this prized favor.

Mimi reached too, but she was too far away to get a coconut. A Zulu cup bounced off her fingers but her mother grabbed it as it rolled to the ground.

After the last float passed, Mimi's father eased her down, and said, "Who wants cotton candy?"

Now Mimi knew what cotton was, and she knew what candy was, but she couldn't imagine cotton candy. They watched the vendor pick up a long, white cone which he spun round and round in a wonderful machine. Mimi could not believe it when lovely pink clouds clung to the cone until it was a big, fluffy ball. She took a huge bite, and the pink cloud melted in her mouth to a drop of sweetness.

COTTON
CANDY

Then the smell of fresh roasted peanuts filled the air. A man strolled by singing:

Peanuts, peanuts, nice and brown.
Makes your lips go up and down.

Father dug into his pocket for some change to buy a bag, and he shelled and ate the crunchy nuts.

Mimi heard sirens again. Her father said, "Here comes Rex, King of Carnival!" as he swooped her up on his shoulders again.

Soon the pink and gold float of Rex glided through the crowd. Everyone was cheering while Rex, on his royal throne, waved his golden scepter. Mimi waved, too, and Rex spotted the little princess perched on her father's shoulders. Rex winked at her and blew her a kiss, which made her feel very special.

Following Rex was a gigantic papier-maché cow with a beautiful garland of flowers woven around its neck.

"That's the Boeuf Gras, or Fat Cow, Mimi," her mother called to her. "It's an old, old, French symbol of Mardi Gras."

"A fat cow on Fat Tuesday," laughed Mimi.

Many more floats passed, and each one seemed more beautiful than the last. There were floats of dragons, flowers, elves, and alligators. The people shouted, "Throw me something, mister!" and the maskers on the floats threw beads, trinkets, and golden coins called doubloons.

Mimi caught some beads, but her parents caught many more. They put the necklaces over her head until she couldn't fit another. And although the beads were pretty and fun to catch, Mimi really wanted a golden doubloon more than anything else in the world. For every float, she raised her hands high trying to catch one, but she never could.

When the last float rolled by, Mimi had an idea. She lifted the crown from her head and held it upside down like a giant cup. She made a wish and with all her might called out, "Throw me something, mister!" Just then, one of the maskers threw out a shower of golden coins. Mimi heard a "kerplunk." In the middle of her crown was what she had wished for — a shiny doubloon! She carefully took it out and hid it in her pocket.

After the parade and decorated trucks passed, Mimi was so tired she napped in the car all the way to her cousin's house where friends and relatives had gathered. They were all in costume too, and sometimes Mimi couldn't tell who they were until she heard their voices or they lifted their masks. When a strange-looking creature with a purple face and silver antennae approached, Mimi hid behind her mother. But then, a familiar voice said, "Don't you know me, Mimi? I'm Uncle Walker, but you can call me 'Uncle Alien' today. How was your day?"

Mimi hugged her "Uncle Alien" and proudly showed him her strands of beads. "It was so much fun! I'll never forget my first Mardi Gras!"

While the adults talked and stirred huge pots of gumbo and jambalaya, the children sat on the floor in a small room. They took out their beads and counted them to see who had the most. Mimi slipped her hand in her pocket and felt her doubloon. She squeezed her fingers around it, closed her eyes, and thought about the exciting day.

After the sun had set, Mimi's father took her hand and told her that it was time to go home. On the ride back, Mimi's father winked at her mother and began to sing:

> If ever I cease to love,
> If ever I cease to love,
> May the moon be turned
> Into green cream cheese,
> If ever I cease to love.

"I've never heard that crazy song before! What is it?" Mimi asked.

Her father answered, "Well, that is the official Mardi Gras song, Mimi. But if you think it's funny, listen to the second verse."

> If ever I cease to love,
> If ever I cease to love,
> May fish grow legs,
> And cows lay eggs,
> If ever I cease to love.

Mimi and her parents laughed and sang the Mardi Gras song all the way home.

As they pulled into their driveway, Mimi sighed, "I'm so sorry that Mardi Gras is over. I wish that it would never end, and I could be a princess forever."

Her mother patted her cheek and said, "No, Mimi, Mardi Gras is a special day which only comes once a year. But don't worry, honey, you'll always be a little princess to us!"